The Treasure of Gunnar Forkbeard

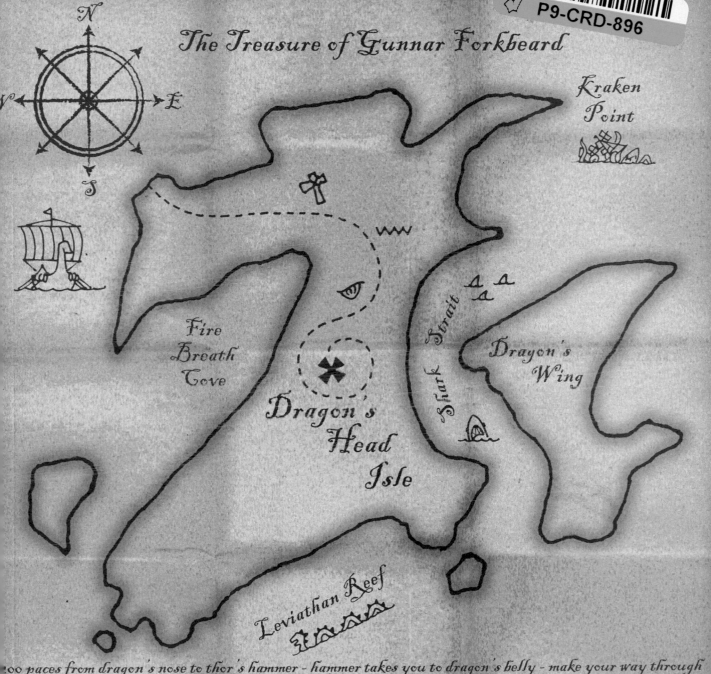

N · E · W · S

Kraken Point

Fire Breath Cove

Shark Strait

Dragon's Wing

Dragon's Head Isle

Leviathan Reef

:oo paces from dragon's nose to thor's hammer - hammer takes you to dragon's belly - make your way through dripping dragon's teeth (beware loose teeth) - the young eye of the dragon will show the way - - follow the descending spiral to the treasure room -

Seamus
(the Famous)

The Treasure of Gunnar Forkbeard

Written and Illustrated by Christopher Ring

Dedicated to Mary Ring
whose son was a daydreamer . . . and she was ok with that.

Bryan Seaton: Publisher
Vito Delsante: Editor In Chief
Jason Martin: Publisher-Danger Zone
Chad Cicconi: First Mate in charge of Mutiny

I'M SO GLAD YOU BOYS ARE HERE.

BESIDES WHAT YOU BRING TO KEEP THE ORPHANAGE GOING, I THINK I HAVE SOMETHING YOU MIGHT FIND INTERESTING.

WHILE WALKING WITH THE CHILDREN, CAMELLIA FOUND IT IN A BOTTLE WASHED UP ON THE BEACH.

MAMA PEARL, DO YOU KNOW WHAT THIS IS?!

I'VE HEARD STORIES SINCE I WAS A LITTLE GIRL.

I'VE GOT A BAD FEELING ABOUT THIS.

NO TIME TO LOSE! MAMA PEARL, THIS COULD KEEP THE ORPHANAGE RUNNING FOREVER!

WAIT, AREN'T WE GOING TO TALK ABOUT THIS?!

SEAMUS??

CAMELLIA?

WEREN'T YOU GOING TO SAY HELLO? ...GOODBYE? ...ANYTHING?

UM...UH... OF COURSE!... IT'S JUST...THAT... THE THING...WITH...THE PIRATE STUFF... AND...UH...

UUUGH! I CAN'T BEAR TO WATCH.

The Salty Barnacle

LATER...

IF WE SET SAIL AT FIRST LIGHT...

WELL, IF IT ISN'T CAP'N SHAMELESS!

OH NO.

IT'S SEAMUS, AND I DON'T HAVE TIME FOR YOUR...

DON'T HAVE TIME FOR PROPER PIRATIN' IS WHAT YA MEAN!

YOUR TREASURE HUNTING AND GIVING TO THE POOR IS GIVING PIRATIN' A BAD NAME.

YOUR NAME COULDN'T GET ANY WORSE, BARRACUDA, AND WE'RE THE BEST PIRATES AROUND.

THEN MAYBE YOU SHOULD PROVE IT WITH A GAME OF PIRATE DARTS!

THIS AGAIN?! FITCHER HAS BEATEN ALL YOUR CREW TEN TIMES OVER.

WE'VE GOT US A NEW CREW MEMBER.

MEET SHURIKEN.

OOOH, A NINJA, HOW MYSTERIOUS.

LET'S DO THIS. WHAT'S THE WAGER?

A DOZEN DUBLOONS PER CREW MEMBER!

DONE!

YOU SURE ABOUT THIS?

UUUUHH... I REALLY DON'T KNOW.

DOES A CHICKEN HAVE LIPS?

EXACTLY.

THE CONTEST IS WEAPON OF CHOICE AT 20 PACES. CLOSEST TO THE BULLSEYE AFTER BOTH HAVE THROWN IS THE WINNER. THE CHALLENGER THROWS FIRST.

SHINNG

THNK

HHUUZZAAAAHHH!!

ALL THE KIDS ARE ASLEEP, MAMA PEARL.

YOU ARE AN ANGEL, CAMELLIA.

I FIXED US TWO PLATES. FIGURED WE'D EAT OUT ON THE PORCH ON SUCH A NICE EVENING.

MMM, SMELLS GOOD, PEARL.

MIND IF WE JOIN YOU?

WE'VE GOT NOTHING FOR YOU HERE, BARRACUDA.

YOU BEST GET TO STEPPIN' BEFORE CAPTAIN SEAMUS AND HIS MEN GET BACK.

THAT'S *CAPTAIN* BARRACUDA!

AND WE KNOW THE KESTREL SET SAIL THIS EVENING. WHAT WE DON'T KNOW IS WHERE THEY'RE HEADING AND WHY.

PERHAPS YOU CAN HELP US WITH THAT.

WE DON'T KNOW ANYTHING ABOUT THAT.

HE'S CARRYING A MESSAGE.

WHAT'S WRONG WITH YOU?!

UUUHH ...*BIRD*

...*CAT*

YOU DO THE MATH.

IT'S BAD NEWS FROM MAMA PEARL. AFTER WE SET SAIL, BARRACUDA AND HIS THUGS RAIDED THE ORPHANGE, FOUND OUT ABOUT FORKBEARD'S TREASURE AND KIDNAPPED CAMELLIA.

SOOO I'M *HEARING*... SINCE WE GOT THE MESSAGE, WE DON'T REALLY *NEED* THE BIR...

YOU'RE NOT...

EATING...

THE BIRD.

FINE! SO WHAT DO WE DO ABOUT BARRACUDA? GO BACK??

NO, HE'LL SPOT US TOO EASILY AT SEA AND CAMELLIA COULD GET HURT IN A BATTLE.

WE'RE A FULL TIDE AHEAD OF HIM, SO WE HAVE TIME TO PREPARE *THE ANGLER*.

LATER...

MASTER FICTHER, DRAGON'S HEAD *HO!*

PREPARE A LONG BOAT AND MAKE READY THE ANCHOR, THERE'S A TREASURE TO BE FOUND!

ROW TOWARDS THE NOSE OF DRAGON'S HEAD, THE MAP STARTS THERE.

AYE, SKIP.

THE MAP SAYS WE TAKE 200 PACES FROM THE NOSE OF DRAGON'S HEAD INTO THE JUNGLE AND LOOK FOR THOR'S HAMMER.

STAY SHARP MATES, I'M SURE GUNNAR FORKBEARD LEFT SOME NASTY SURPRISES FOR US.

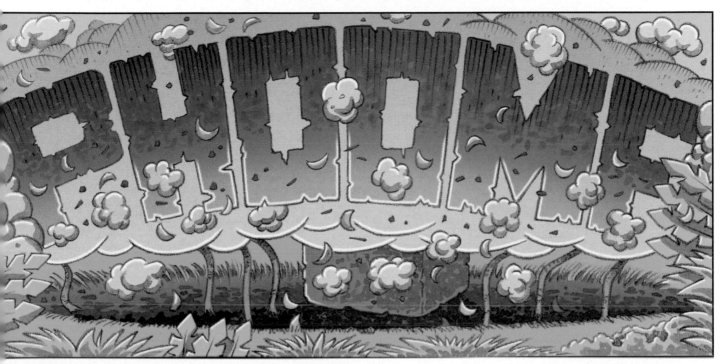

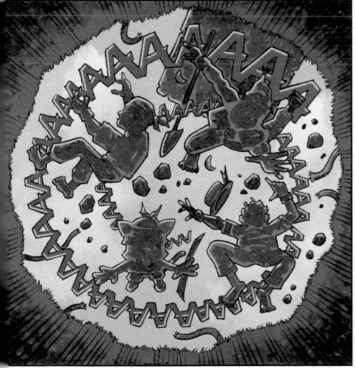

THERE SHE IS, THE GREYTHORN.

BACK ON THE HIGH SEAS

NOW TO TAKE THE ANGLER DOWN AND GET UNDER HER.

HAVE TO COME UP ON HER HULL QUIETLY.

OSMUNDA! YOU FOUND ME!

HE'S GOING TO *WHAT?!*

ABOARD THE GREYTHORN

ZZ ZZ ZZ ZZ ZZ

PUHUUUUH PANT... PANT... PANT...

HOOO... MIGHT... NEED TO WORK... ON MY CARDIO.

FWOOOSSHH

CAMELLIA?

CAMELLIA? IT'S SEAMUS. CAMELLIA?

SEAMUS, THIS WAY. I'M LOCKED IN HERE.

DON'T WORRY, CAMELLIA, I'LL GET YOU OUT.

HURRY, THE KEY IS HANGING ON THE POST BY THE STAIRS.

HURRY, THIS WAY.

CAPTAIN SEAMUS IS ABOARD THE GREYTHORN!

AARRGH!

AARRGH!

HE'S AFTER THE GIRL.

ALL HANDS BELOW DECK!

AARRGH!

QUICKLY, DOWN HERE.

AARRGH!

WHERE BE THE RUNT?!

PREPARE TO CAST OFF!

UUH... NOT A PIRATE, I'VE NO IDEA WHAT THAT MEANS!

IT MEANS PEDAL, AND FAST!

POP

WAROOOOSSH

RRUUUUNN!!!

LOOKS LIKE THE TRAIL OF TEETH LEADS TO THIS OPEN CHAMBER, SKIP.

"WHERE THE YOUNG EYE OF THE DRAGON WILL SHOW THE WAY".

LOOK SKIP, THE EYE'S LIGHT...

"...SHINES RIGHT...

...TO THAT TUNNEL."

LET'S GO!

BUT WHY THE "YOUNG" EYE?

WAIT!

STAND BACK.

PLINK

SSSSCCRRRREEEEEEEEEE

DAWN...

FITCHER AND THE CREW MADE SHORE HERE. FROM WHAT I REMEMBER OF THE MAP WE SHOULD BE ABLE TO CATCH UP TO THEM.

LOOK ALIVE, GENTS! FIRST LIGHT IS UPON US AND TREASURE AWAITS.

YAWN AYE, SKIP.

AYE, SKIP.

AYE, SKIP.

JUST A WEE BIT MORE AAAND...

...BINGO!

BUT SKIPPER, THERE'S NOTHING THERE. NO OPENING OR NOTHING!

YA KNOW, I GIVE YOU *ONE* JOB AND THIS IS WHAT I FIND.

A CAPTAIN'S WORK...

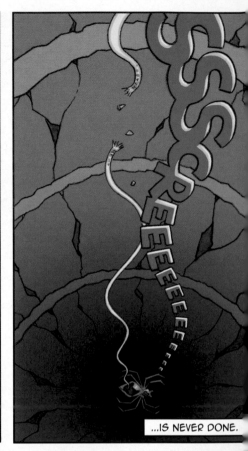

SSSCREEEEEEEEEEP!

...IS NEVER DONE.

NOW, IF YOU'RE DONE HANGIN' AROUND DOWN THERE, I WAS THINKING ABOUT, OH, I DON'T KNOW... MAYBE GOING TO FIND SOME TREASURE.

WHAT D'YA SAY?

OH SURE, IT'S *EASY* WHEN I LEAVE YOU A TRAIL TO FOLLOW!

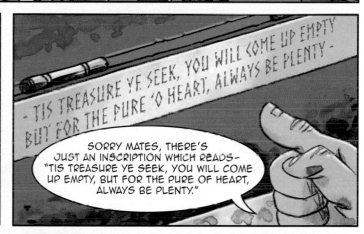

FITCHER, YOU KEPT THE EMPTY CHEST?

YEP, IT'S STILL A BOX AND III'M STILL A CAT.

WE'LL MAKE OUR WAY BACK TO THE KESTREL, AND FITCHER..?

WHAT?!

STOP POUTING.

THBBPTH!

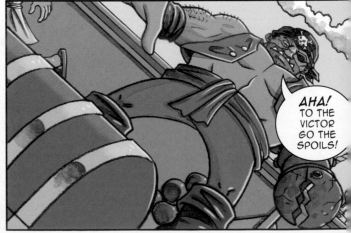

EMPTY??!

IS THIS SOME KIND OF TRICK?!

NO TRICK, PIRATES' BARGAIN, THE GIRL FOR THE CHEST. THE CHEST WAS EMPTY WHEN WE FOUND IT.

THEN WE'LL BE TAKING BACK THE GIRL, BARGAIN UR NU BARGAIN!

UH, YEAH THAT'S...

...NOT GONNA...

...HAPPEN!

WHOA, THIS SHIP JUST GOT REAL.

SO, 'TIS A SCRAP THE LITTLE FURBALL WANTS? OBLIGE HIM, MATEYS.

CAN YOU TAKE THEM?

MEH... FOUGHT BIGGER, NOT UGLIER.

IF WE WERE IN A SANDBOX MY INSTINCT WOULD BE TO COVER THEM UP.

AARRGH!

AARRGH!

GRRR!

HHHSSSSSSS!

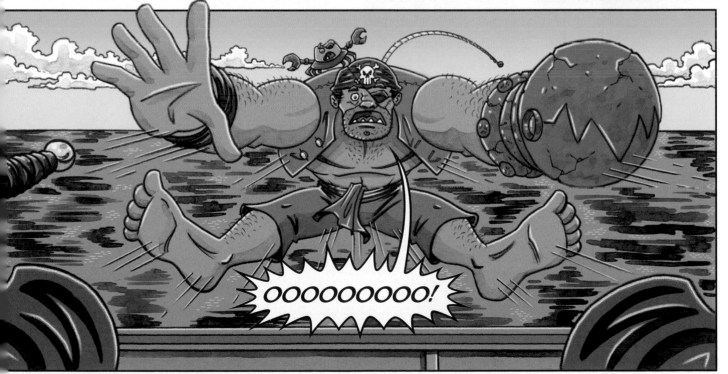

The End

About the Author . . .

   Christopher Ring has been an illustrator and designer for over 25 years. His clients include Ad Agencies, Trading and Greeting Card Companies, The Textile Industry, Medical Fields, Promotional Specialties and Libraries. He entered into the comics arena with his creator owned series "CarbonKnight" which led to work with both independent and veteran publishers. His first foray into Childrens' Books was the Halloween tale "The Scariest Creature". With "Seamus (the Famous)", Chris has woven together the best of both worlds by combining the fast paced action and comedic timing of sequential art with the charm and magic of Children's Books. He plans to write and illustrate many more adventures with Seamus and Fitcher while residing in Pennsylvania with his wife and children.

To follow Chris's appearnces and work online go to:
www.facebook.com/chrisringillustrator
or on Instagram ring1459

BEHIND THE SCENES OF "SEAMUS (THE FAMOUS)"

A LOT OF WORK IS DONE BEFORE EVEN ONE PAGE OF FINISHED ART IS COMPLETE. HERE'S A GLIMPSE AT SOME OF THE THUMBNAILS AND MODEL SHEETS THAT WENT INTO CREATING THE STORY. YOU MAY NOTICE HOW THE CHARACTERS EVOLVED FROM THESE INITIAL SKETCHES.

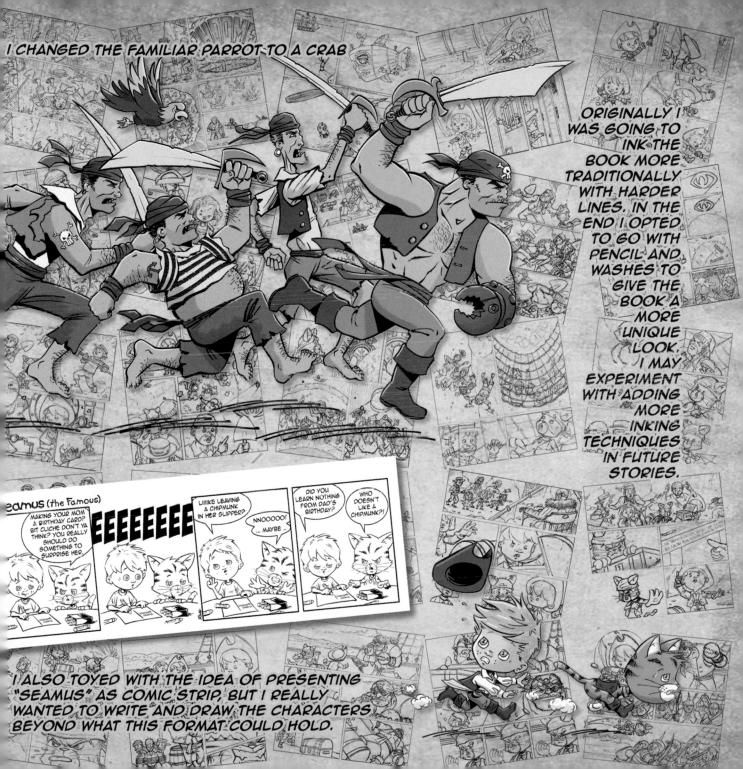

I CHANGED THE FAMILIAR PARROT-TO A CRAB

ORIGINALLY I WAS GOING TO INK THE BOOK MORE TRADITIONALLY WITH HARDER LINES. IN THE END I OPTED TO GO WITH PENCIL AND WASHES TO GIVE THE BOOK A MORE UNIQUE LOOK. I MAY EXPERIMENT WITH ADDING MORE INKING TECHNIQUES IN FUTURE STORIES.

eamus (the Famous)

MAKING YOUR MOM A BIRTHDAY CARD? BIT CLICHE DON'T YA THINK? YOU REALLY SHOULD DO SOMETHING TO SURPRISE HER.

EEEEEEEE

LIIIIKE LEAVING A CHIPMUNK IN HER SLIPPER?

NNOOOOO! ... MAYBE ..

DID YOU LEARN NOTHING FROM DAD'S BIRTHDAY?

WHO DOESN'T LIKE A CHIPMUNK?!

I ALSO TOYED WITH THE IDEA OF PRESENTING "SEAMUS" AS COMIC STRIP, BUT I REALLY WANTED TO WRITE AND DRAW THE CHARACTERS BEYOND WHAT THIS FORMAT COULD HOLD.